I have this little sister Lola.
She is small and very funny.

Sometimes for a treat,
Mum says, "We are going to
the shops and you may choose
one thing."

"One thing EACH," I say,
      "or ONE thing
              between TWO?"

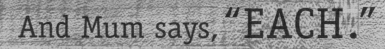

And Mum says, "EACH."

I say to Lola,
"We are going to the shops and we are allowed to choose ONE thing."

"One thing to **share**?" says Lola.

I say,
"One thing EACH,
which means TWO actual things."

"**Two things?**" says Lola.

"TWO things **between** TWO," I say.

Mum says we must be ready in TEN minutes.

It takes me THREE minutes to clean my teeth,

ONE minute to remember that I have forgotten to eat breakfast,

FOUR minutes to eat my puffa pops,

Lola shouts,
"I just need to do **something**."

I say,
"WHAT thing?"

She says,
"**One** thing."

I say,
"But we don't
have time..."

She says,
"I will be **half** of
a **second**."

after TWO whole minutes, which is in fact 120 SECONDS, this is NOT TRUE because

I go into our room to find Lola.

"What are you DOING?" I say.

Lola says,

"I am just trying to count the dots on my dress. But I am NOT sure what comes after twelve."

I am running like mad and

Lola is counting ladybirds

on the path.

She says,

"There are
at least FIFTY
or
twenty-seventeen.

How **many** shoes would **FIFTY** or **twenty**-SEVENTEEN ladybirds **need**, Charlie?"

I say, "NONE, ladybirds DON'T WEAR SHOES."

"What about **socks**?" says Lola.

"No, they **NEVER** wear socks."

"It must be **very ouchy**," says Lola.

When we walk past the water meadow
we are followed by several ducks.

"How **many** ducks are **following** us?" asks Lola.

"THREE," I say.

Lola finds half a biscuit
in her coat pocket and starts
feeding them crumbs.

"How many **now**?"
she says.

I say,
"THREE ducks,
SEVEN pigeons,
FIVE wading birds,
FOUR swans,
TWO geese and
ONE flapping bird."

3 + 7 + 5 + 4 + 2 + 1 = 22

"Run!"

shouts Lola.

Lola looks up at the sky and she says,
"Look at all of **those** singing birds – there are

one two five SEVEN twenty
sixteen eleventeen NINE birds singing."

1   2

are

there

And I say, "NO, Lola,

I say,
"Well, if you are
so good at counting,
then how many **leaves**
are there on that tree?"

"A **hundred**," says Lola,
"nearly at **least**."

I say,
"There are
MORE THAN
a **hundred**,
more than
A THOUSAND,
even."

"How many is a **thousand**?" says Lola.

"TEN HUNDREDS make A THOUSAND," I say.

$$10 \times 100 = 1000$$

"And is a **thousand** the **most**?" says Lola.

I say, "No, then there is a MILLION and that is

"And is a **million** MORE than the **rain**?" says Lola.

"...or **maybe** even a TRILLION."

"Or a

squi

a THOUSAND times **more**."

"No, the rain is probably a **billion**," I say,

lion?"

says Lola.

I say,
"I don't know if a
SQUILLION is a **number**."

It takes us **another** ONE HUNDRED and fifty-si

When we get there, Mum says, "You may choose one thing."

And Lola says,

"**Three** things."

3

steps to walk to the shops. **156**

And Mum says,
"ONE thing."

1

And Lola says,
"**Two** things."

2

And Mum says,
"How about NO things?"

O

And Lola says,
"How
about
one
thing?"

And Mum says,
"All right, ONE thing."

And Lola says,

"Yes, **One** thing."

I spend THREE minutes looking at the comics
and TWO minutes looking at the badges and
I make up my mind in FIVE seconds.

I choose the
SIX badges.

Lola is still looking.

After **ELEVEN** minutes, Mum says,
"Hurry up, Lola, we are leaving in
one minute."

TWO minutes later, Lola chooses **twelve** stickers.

On the way home, Lola sticks FIVE stickers on the **pavement**, THREE on a **tree** and TWO on her **shoes**, ONE on **me** ... she even sticks ONE on Marv's **dog**.

By the time we get to our flat there are NO stickers left.

NONE.

12 - 5 - 3 - 2 - 1 - 1 = 0